FLIGHT OF THE SPACE QUESTER

BY JOHN BIANCHI

The stars! Awesome beacons of light in an infinite darkness of wonder! Since the dawn of creation, Earthlings have looked upward and dreamed of a voyage into this shemozzle of space, matter and time.

The Bungalo Boys have been observers of the celestial void for many years. Now it is time to put their knowledge as amateur astronomers to good use. Tomorrow, they will ride one of the Earth's most exciting space vehicles: the **Space Quester**!

Before bed, the boys engage in some last-minute preparations:

To ease the tension, Johnny-Bob does some speed work on the Astrocycle.

Rufus — a self-taught astrophysicist — looks over some final rocket research.

The Big Book of ROCKETS

A fanatic for detail, Curly pores over his star charts one last time.

Little Shorty and Projectile the Wonder Dog continue to work on their eye-hand coordination.

Dawn breaks, and the boys treat themselves to a carefully planned preflight meal. Curly, Rufus, Johnny-Bob and Little Shorty each eat something from one of the four major food groups.

Curly chooses the Whole Grains and Cereal Food Group.

Johnny-Bob prefers the Whole Donut Food Group.

Rufus makes a wise choice from the Microwave Food Group.

Little Shorty and Pro share a selection from the Dairy Food Group.

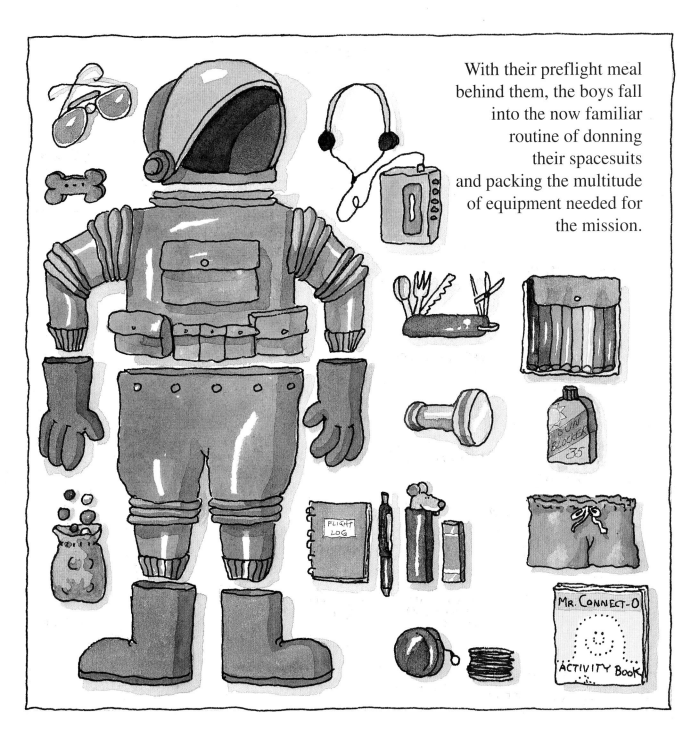

With their preflight meal behind them, the boys fall into the now familiar routine of donning their spacesuits and packing the multitude of equipment needed for the mission.

Once the crew members are suited up, Ma Bungalo drives them to the launch site in the astronaut transporter.

The boys are wonderstruck as they approach the Space Quester!

Lift-off is surprisingly slow, but the great space machine rattles ever upward through the thunderheads. As the Space Quester clears the last of the clouds, Little Shorty begins to question his ability to complete the mission.

As the launch vehicle reaches apogee, it turns and plunges back toward Earth. The Space Quester will now use gravity — one of nature's most dangerous forces — to boost the craft's already awesome speed.

Once under way, the boys waste no time getting down to work.

| Curly records his observations photographically. | Rufus makes an entry in his flight log. | Little Shorty performs an experiment relating to centrifugal force. |

Nearing the halfway point
of the mission, Little Shorty takes
an unscheduled spacewalk . . .

. . . and Projectile has a chance
to deploy the newly redesigned
BungleArm™.

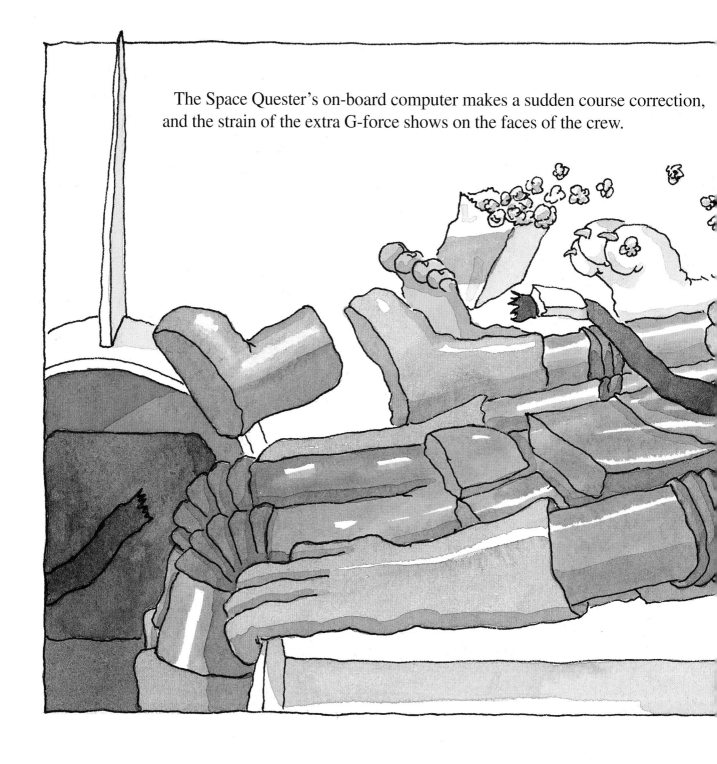

The Space Quester's on-board computer makes a sudden course correction, and the strain of the extra G-force shows on the faces of the crew.

After their trajectory has been successfully corrected, the boys
recall Ma Bungalo's theories on space sickness and preflight meals.

Then, after a final word to Mission Control, the boys are off to explore The Unknown Black Hole.

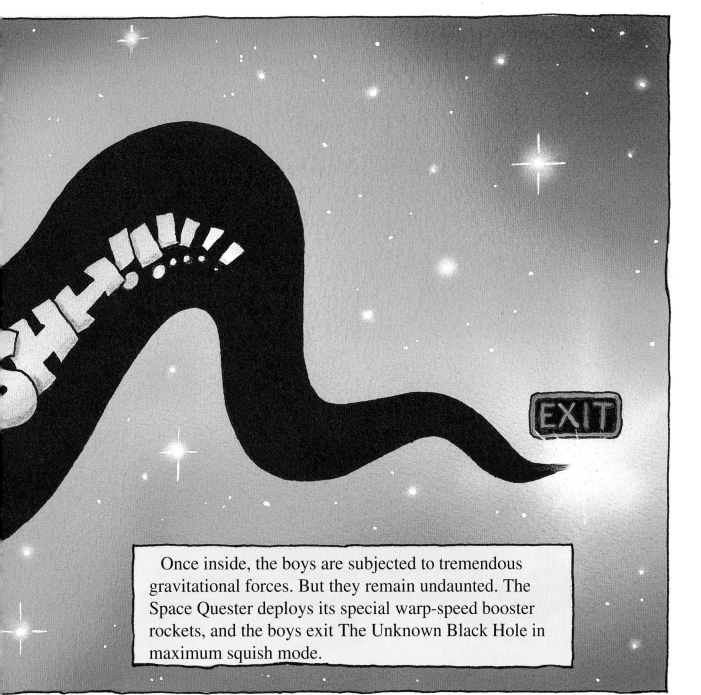

Once inside, the boys are subjected to tremendous gravitational forces. But they remain undaunted. The Space Quester deploys its special warp-speed booster rockets, and the boys exit The Unknown Black Hole in maximum squish mode.

With impeccable timing, the on-board computers fire the ship's retro-rockets, and the boys prepare for splashdown. The Space Quester's multiple nose cones glow with the blazing heat of atmospheric reentry.

To slow the craft's mind-boggling speed, Little Shorty hastily deploys the emergency drag chute . . .

. . . and the Space Quester makes a flawless three-point landing — through the Swan Pond!

In what seems like an instant, the flight of the Space Quester is over. The boys are met by excited technicians who help them exit their vehicle.

The Bungalo Boys are anxious to share their scientific findings, but first they must locate the food court for the traditional postflight meal.